W9-CNB-896

the Raindrop

Brian D. McClure

Illustrated by Buddy Plumlee

UNIVERSAL FLAG PUBLISHING • LISLE, ILLINOIS

The Raindrop
Copyright © 2006 by Brian D. McClure

Published by Universal Flag Publishing,
a division of Universal Flag, Ltd.

Illustrations by Buddy Plumlee
Cover design by Aretta Swanson
Cover illustrations by Buddy Plumlee
Page layout/production by 224 Creative, LLC

All rights reserved.
No part of this book may be reproduced or transmitted in any form or by any means,
electronic or mechanical, including photocopying, recording, or by any information storage
and retrieval system, without written permission from the publisher, except for the inclusion
of brief quotations in a review.

For Information contact:

Universal Flag Publishing
PO Box 4354
Lisle, IL 60532
(630) 245-8500
e-mail: publishing@UniversalFlag.com

ISBN-13   978-1-933426-01-3
ISBN-10   1-933426-01-2

If you are unable to order this book from your local bookseller,
you may order directly from the publisher. Quantity discounts
are available. Call Universal Flag Publishing at (630) 245-8500.

Printed in China

10 9 8 7 6 5 4 3 2 1

*My dedication is to you, in honor of the
great gifts you bring to our world!*

Thank you for who you are!

Brian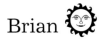

I am just a raindrop; I am smaller than small.
What am I doing here? I have no use at all...

"What are you talking about?" asked the Cloud, "You are part of the water system, and you should be proud."

"No," said the Raindrop, "I am sure you are wrong. I am good for nothing, and soon I'll be gone."

"I know your problem," the Cloud said in reply. "I can do nothing to help you, I can only stand by. However, before you go, there is something I would like you to know. Without you, there would be no life on earth. I urge you to rethink, the state of your worth!"

The Raindrop didn't listen, and soon let go of the Cloud. As it fell through the sky, it repeated its cry. "I am smaller than small; I am no use at all." The Raindrop's every thought, was of what it was not. As a result, the Raindrop could not see, hear, or feel anything else.

At the same time all this was going on, the earth had its own problems. It had not rained in months. The leaves on the trees had long since fallen, and the grass on the ground was browner than brown. Animals and insects were dying by the day, how long they would last, no one could say. If it did not rain soon, all would be lost. The earth and its inhabitants needed water, at any cost. "Please rain, please rain, oh please rain," was the call. It was not uttered by a few, it was uttered by ALL!

As the Raindrop fell, it was surrounded by millions of other drops. All of them answering the call for help; all of them that is, except for the Raindrop. The Raindrop was only concerned with itself.

Drop by drop the water hit the ground; to all the earth it was a beautiful sound. From the fish to the trees, and the soil and the bees, everything rejoiced in a song of thanks.

When the Raindrop hit the ground it had no idea what was happening. It found itself surrounded by water, and heading down through rocks, soil, roots, and sand. All of a sudden one thing was clear; the Raindrop was flooded with nothing but fear. It looked to its left and it looked to its right, it could see nothing, it was darker than night! "Where am I?" the Raindrop cried, and where am I going it wondered inside? There was no answer that the Raindrop could hear, and that only increased the Raindrop's fear.

In the meantime, the water continued to pour from the sky. The lakes and streams were filling, where once they had been dry. Nature was springing to life again; soon things would be normal since the drought was at an end. Everywhere there was a sound that was heard that day; it was the sound of everything, in its own unique way.

Can you guess the sound
    that was heard everywhere that day?

    I'll give you a clue; it is inside of you,
        and it is something that you love to do!

LAUGH!

A prayer of laughter could be heard all over that day, in honor of the water that was sent the earth's way! Happiness was absolutely everywhere to be found, except with the Raindrop, which was far under ground!

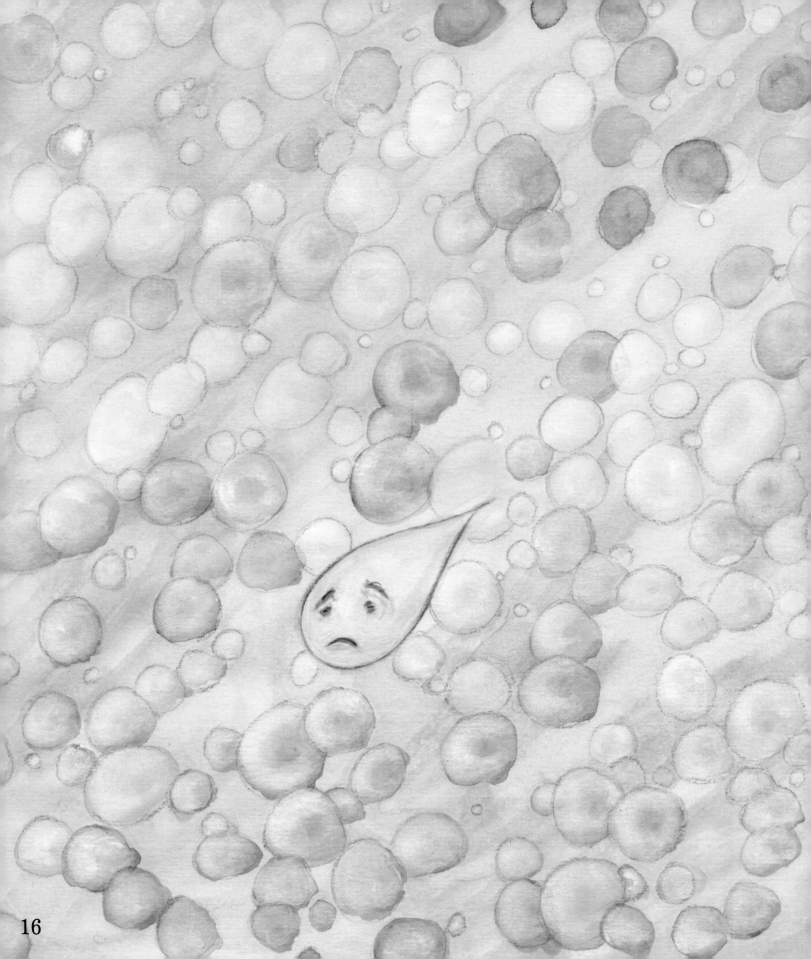

The Raindrop found itself coming to a stop; it was surrounded by water, from the bottom to the top. For the first time since this adventure began, the Raindrop asked the water a question. "Where are we?" Silence was all that the Raindrop heard. Day after day it continued that way. Days turned into weeks, and weeks turned into months, and still nothing happened. The Raindrop had long since stopped talking, thinking, or feeling; it was sure that it would spend the rest of its life all alone.

Then one day there was a loud sound, and the Raindrop was pulled, from way underground. Up and up and up it was pulled, where it was going, it had not been told.

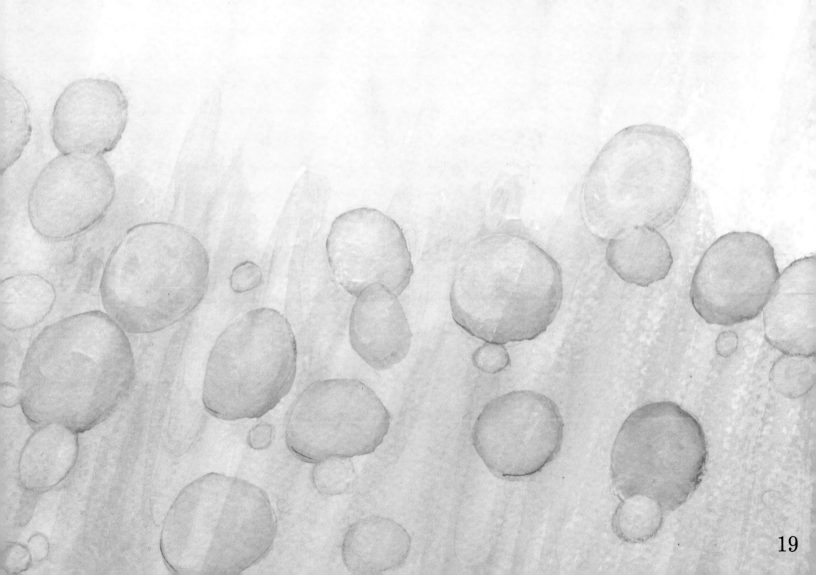

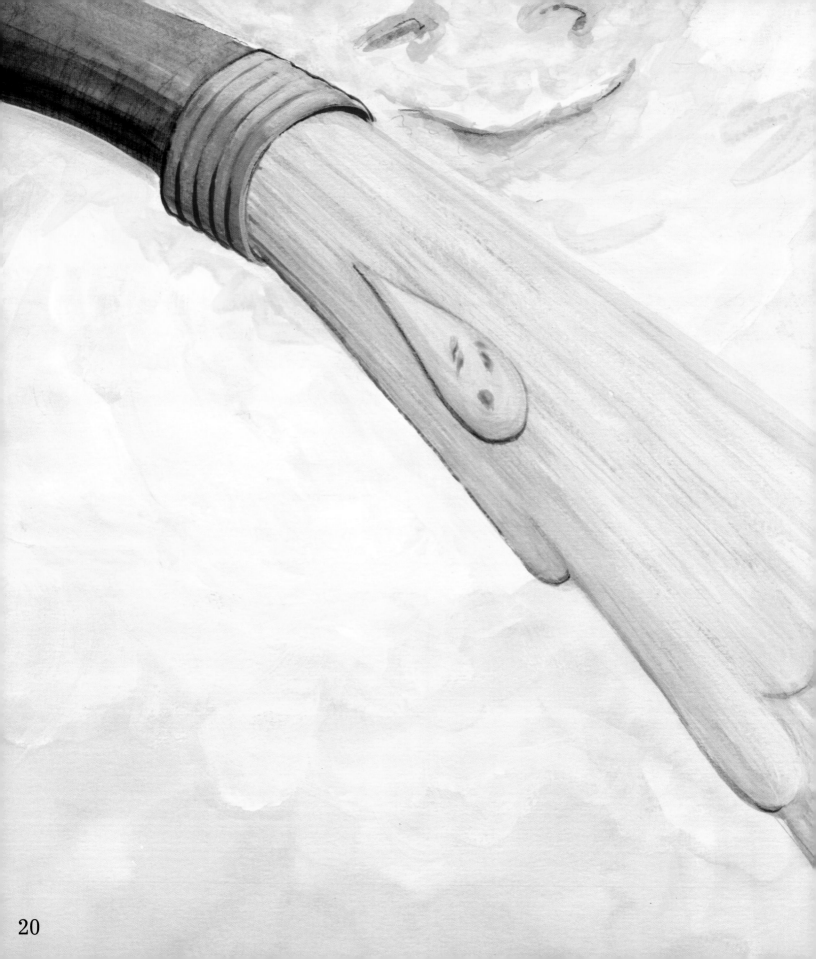

Within seconds the Raindrop flew out of a hose, it was covered in light from its head to its toes. It happened so fast, in the blink of an eye, that the Raindrop had no time, to laugh or cry. Blinded at first by the rays of the sun, the Raindrop allowed the adjustment to come. "Oh my, oh my, what a beautiful day." Those were the only words that the Raindrop, had time to say.

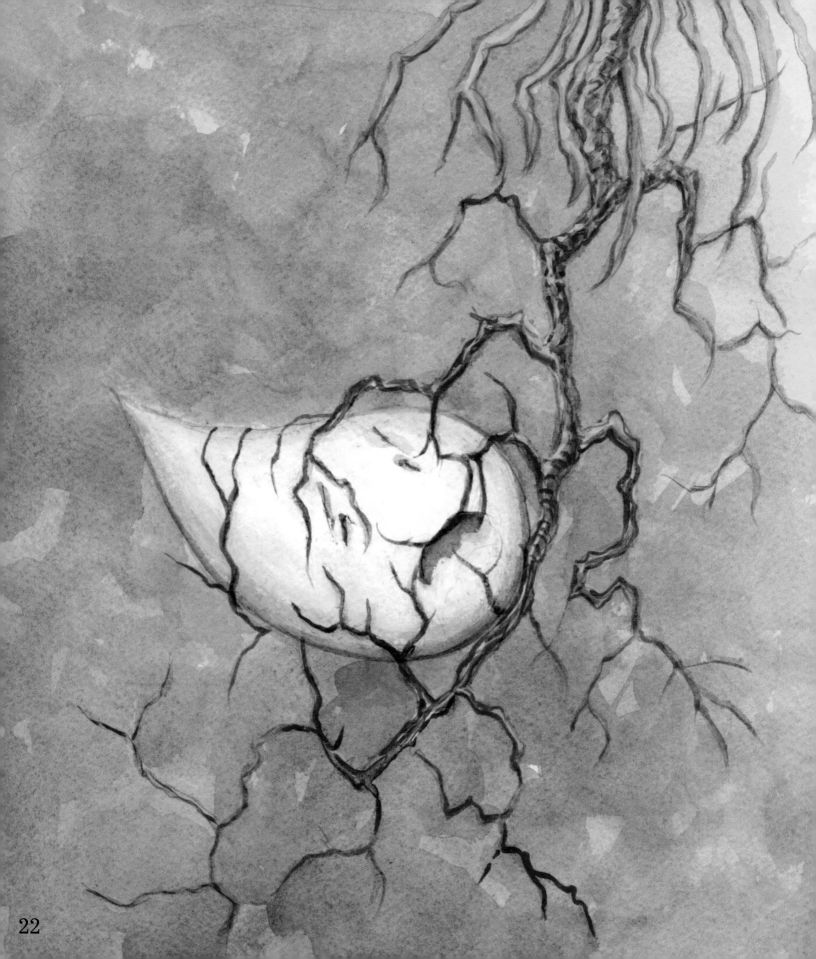

As fast as the daylight had appeared it was gone, and the Raindrop found itself sinking with the water again. Through the rocks, soil, and then, just like that, the roots, grabbed onto the water, that was passing by. "I'm stuck." said the Raindrop, and it started to cry.

Then all of a sudden from out of the blue, there was the sun again, what an unbelievable view. So surprised was the Raindrop it had nothing to say; all it could do was admire the day. The corn had absorbed the water so quick, pulled it up through its stalk and started the clock.

Soon after, the Raindrop noticed a sound, curious enough, it looked all around. There was a well, a farmer, and a hose; and corn everywhere, by the rows and rows.

The farmer was pumping water, direct from the well, and it sprayed on the corn, from the hose as it fell. The corn soaked up the water as fast as it could, while the soil added minerals just as it should. The sun added light and heat to the mix, and just like that, the Raindrop saw through its fix.

It was in that very instant that the Raindrop knew, the deep hidden truth, once hidden from view. The Raindrop realized it had never been alone; as a matter of fact, it had always been home. "I am part of the water system." the Raindrop cried out. "Why didn't I see that?" it asked with a shout. What happened next was the best of all, the Raindrop let out its own unique call! Laughter! The Raindrop laughed and laughed, sending out its thanks to all!

The sun continued to shine on the corn and soon the Raindrop's purpose was complete. Before it could say goodbye to the day, it was broken into smaller particles. Some of the Raindrop became hydrogen, some of it became oxygen, and some of it became the corn. Through the wonderful process of energy, the Raindrop changed form.

But that is not the end of the story!

No one can say how long it was; all they can do
is confirm that it happened this way.

One day two parts of hydrogen and one part of oxygen met up in a cloud. They came together as one, and then laughed out loud! If you haven't guessed it already, you might as well know, the Raindrop was back, and ready to go. This time the Raindrop remembered much more, it knew the oneness of all, and the gifts we all share. It knew if we did not all work as one, nothing would exist, not even the sun!

Just as the Raindrop stopped laughing, it heard the cloud utter this cry, "I am just a cloud, up in the sky, I am no use at all, oh me, oh my. Why am I here? What can I do? I have no purpose for living, I wish I were through."

The Raindrop smiled in recognition of the plea, and comforted the cloud with a smile of glee. "What are you talking about?" asked the drop. "You are part of the process of life, and not just a prop!"

"No," said the cloud," I am sure you are wrong. I am good for nothing, and soon I'll be gone."

"I know your problem," the drop said in reply. "I can do nothing to help you, I can only stand by..."

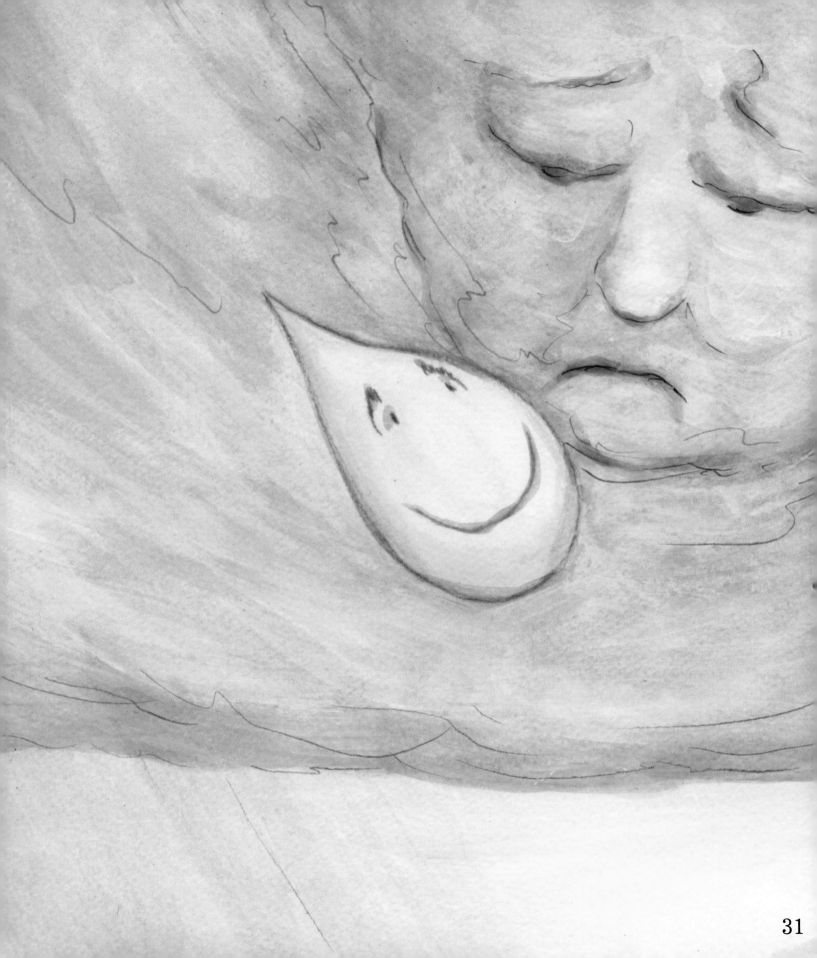

*And now for You! Before you go, there are
a few things the Raindrop and I would like you to know.*

You are a Great Gift to the World!

You are Loved every second of every day!

You are One with everything there is!

*We are looking forward to seeing you soon.
Thank you for reading, "Our Story!"*

The Beginning

33